Fortunately,
UNFORTUNATELY

For Klaus, my publisher . . .
fortunately

First American edition published in 2011 by Andersen Press USA, an imprint of Andersen Press Ltd.
www.andersenpressusa.com
First published in Great Britain in 2010 by Andersen Press Ltd.,
20 Vauxhall Bridge Road, London SW1V 2SA.
Published in Australia by Random House Australia Pty.,
Level 3, 100 Pacific Highway, North Sydney, NSW 2060.

Copyright © Michael Foreman, 2010.
Jacket illustrations copyright © Michael Foreman, 2010.

Distributed in the United States and Canada by
Lerner Publishing Group, Inc.
241 First Avenue North
Minneapolis, MN 55401 U.S.A.
www.lernerbooks.com

Color separated in Switzerland by Photolitho AG, Zürich.
Printed and bound in Singapore by Tien Wah Press.
Michael Foreman has used watercolor paints in this book.

Library Cataloging-in-Publication Data available.
ISBN 978-0-7613-7460-2

1 – TWP – 7/2/10
This book has been printed on acid-free paper

Fortunately, UNFORTUNATELY

MICHAEL FOREMAN

ANDERSEN PRESS USA

"Milo! Milo!"

It was Mom.

"Granny has left her umbrella here.
Can you take it to her house, please?"

Fortunately,

it was a lovely day

and Milo liked going to Granny's house because she always had cake…

Fortunately,

he had Granny's umbrella…

Unfortunately,

a dark cloud appeared and it soon began to rain ...

Unfortunately,

he didn't look where he was going...

Fortunately,

the umbrella was

like a parachute…

Unfortunately, there was a whale...

Fortunately,
the umbrella kept Milo afloat inside the whale
and there was a wonderful pirate ship ...

Unfortunately,
the pirate captain was not very friendly …

Fortunately,
he was not very good at sword fighting either ...

Unfortunately, his pipe fell on the gunpowder ...

Fortunately, Milo flew out of the whale's mouth…

Unfortunately, he was caught up in a HURRICANE…

...and dropped into a
lost world at the top of
a volcano.

Fortunately, he splashed down in the blue waters of a lake ...

Unfortunately,
it was full of wild dinosaurs …

Fortunately, the volcano erupted and Milo was thrown

up into the sky again . . .

Unfortunately, he was captured by an alien spaceship ...

Fortunately, the aliens were very tiny—and friendly ...

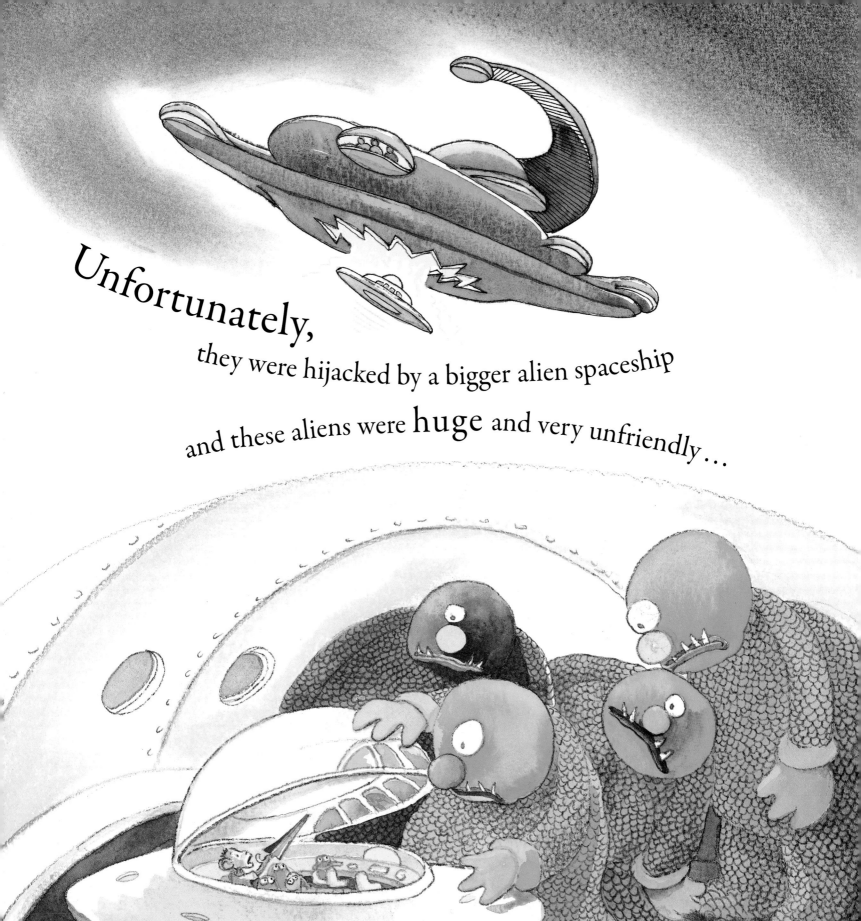

Unfortunately, they were hijacked by a bigger alien spaceship and these aliens were **huge** and very unfriendly...

Fortunately, they were just full of hot air and popped easily, like **big** smelly balloons...

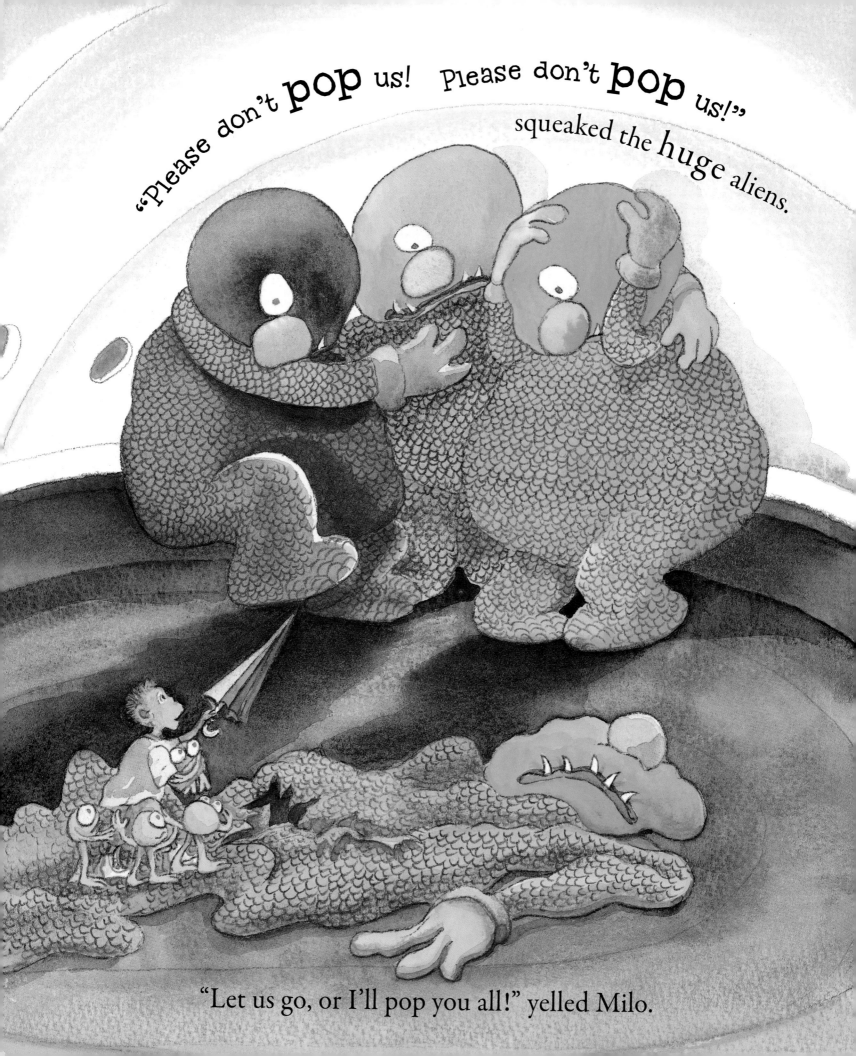

"Go! Go!" the huge aliens cried.

Fortunately, the little aliens flew Milo all the way to . . .

Granny's house ...

Unfortunately, Granny's umbrella was now a bit of a mess.

"What have you done to my umbrella?"

Fortunately, it was full of pirate treasure . . .

Unfortunately, there was also a little alien . . .

Fortunately, his friends came back for him ...

And they all had cake . . .

Unfortunately . . .

"Come on, mateys!
The old lady has got
our treasure . . ."